the nest before christmas

Piper Rayne

Cover Design and Illustrator:

1st Line Editor: Joy Editing

2nd Line Editor: My Brother's Editor

Proofreader: My Brother's Editor

2nd Proofreader: Olivia Winston

about the nest
before christmas

A grounded plane. A questionable Greyhound bus. A brotherhood on a mission.

When the team's plane gets grounded right before Christmas, the Falcons will stop at nothing to make it home for the holidays, including launching their own *Planes, Trains, and Automobiles*-style mission across the country to get back to their wives and kids.

Meanwhile, their wives are back in Chicago, juggling babies, pregnancy tests, and a missing gender-reveal envelope.

From FaceTime flirting gone wrong to a Greyhound bus disaster, the guys' determination never wavers—because nothing says love like a man sprinting through a snowstorm to make it home before Christmas.

The Nest BEFORE CHRISTMAS

one

Jade

Christmas carols play softly in the waiting room—almost as if the doctor's office thinks it will fill the other women and me with holiday cheer. Pretty hard to accomplish when my to-do list is a mile long, but this is what I wanted, right? The happily-ever-after with the man I love and the family we're building. I feel like the Grinch with how stressed and annoyed I am, when so many people are going without, especially this time of year.

The door to the hallway that leads to the exam rooms opens, and all of us waiting women glance up, hope filling us that we're next to be called. Everyone wants to get their appointment over with so they can move on with their tasks for the day.

Thankfully, the nurse calls my name. Guess I'm the lucky one. If I weren't five months pregnant, I'd hop up and run over to her, afraid she'd called the wrong person.

But this is what happens at the OB-GYN office—babies need to be delivered, so we wait because we want the doctor there at the hospital when our little bundles are born too.

"Hello, Jade." Even the nurse has Christmas spirit—her scrubs are covered in tiny Santas. "How are you today?"

My hand runs over my stomach as I shift my purse higher on my shoulder. "Finally warming up from outside."

She glances over her shoulder as she leads me to the dreaded scale at the end of the hall. "Is it still coming down out there?"

"It's tapering off now, but I heard we're due for another few inches before it stops."

"Good for the kids, I suppose. A white Christmas, snowmen, snow forts." She stands beside the scale, waiting. "It's all ready when you are."

I set my purse and coat on the table. I'd love to bend down and unlace these boots. That'd knock off five pounds, maybe seven. "I'm never quite ready to step on a scale."

She chuckles, clearly used to the joke made by almost every woman who comes through this office.

I watch the number climb higher, reminding myself that this is a good thing. I'm making a home for our baby. Still, when I see the final number, my stomach drops. It's such a weird feeling to have no control over all the changes happening to my body.

"Yeah, those Christmas cookies are yummy," I mutter. "And packed with calories, apparently."

She laughs again. "Let's get you to the exam room. The doctor is just returning from a delivery and will be here in about five minutes."

She escorts me into one of the rooms, checks my vitals, and tells me to wait.

I scroll through my texts from Henry where he apologizes again and again for being delayed at an away game and for missing today. He thanks me for waiting to find out the sex of our baby. What else would I do? Where would I be without him? This is our life. This is the unpredictability of him working in the NHL. One storm can change every player's plans.

I send back a heart emoji, tell him I love him, and that we'll celebrate together as soon as he gets home.

A knock sounds on the door and my doctor walks in. She glances at the empty guest chair and frowns. "No Henry? I suspected, since I heard the Falcons away game was postponed."

I give her a small smile. "Yeah. Unfortunately, the game was delayed, so they're playing tonight. Do you think you can determine the sex of the baby today and write it on a piece of paper and put it in an envelope so we can open it together when he gets home?"

"Of course." She pats my knee. "You're not the first I've done that for, and you won't be the last. I know how excited you both are to find out."

"Turns out I'm a planner when it comes to things like this, which is odd, because I would've thought I'd want it to be a surprise."

As she washes her hands at the sink, she looks at me over her shoulder. "I was the same. As soon as I could find out, I did." She grabs the paper towels and dries her hands. "Any plans for Christmas?"

"We rented a big cabin with our friends.

We're going for a long weekend, right before the holidays."

"A little getaway before the chaos, huh?"

I laugh. "It's made my Christmas list ten times longer, unfortunately. Now I have to pack and have everything set for when we return."

She grins. "It's good to get away. This is actually my last day before Christmas. I'll be completely off, no on-call or anything. My husband demanded we go on a vacation. We're going to be away for the entire holiday."

My eyes widen because, as long as Henry's with the Falcons or another team in the league, that's not an option for us. "That's amazing. Where are you going?"

"I wish I could say somewhere without snow, but he loves skiing, so we're heading to the mountains. I'll be in the hot tub or in front of the fire with a book."

"Sounds nice." My voice is a little wistful. As fun as being at the cabin with our friends will be, it won't be as relaxing as her getaway sounds.

"Don't sound too jealous. My entire family will be with us. My parents, his parents, our siblings, and all the kids. It'll be chaotic."

"Built-in babysitters." I shrug.

She grins. "Yup." She rolls her stool over. "But back to you. How are you feeling? Any questions or concerns?"

"Everything's been good." And it has, which makes me think I could do this again soon. I've been blessed with a great pregnancy so far.

She dims the lights, squeezes the jelly onto my stomach, and starts the ultrasound. I'm not sure if it's the darkness, the feel of the cool jelly, or the wand running around my stomach, but I blink away tears. It's silly to be sad, but I really wanted Henry here. He would be if he could, and I remind myself it hurts him not to be here just as much as it does me, so I need to be strong right now.

I force myself not to look at the screen. I want us to see the pictures together, to read the girl or boy on the paper at the same time.

The room fills with the sound of a strong, steady heartbeat and the tears I was forcing back spill down the sides of my face to the paper under me. Hearing the life I'm growing inside me never gets old.

"You're doing a great job," she says warmly. "Everything looks good."

Relief floods me. Not that I thought anything was wrong, but the confirmation is re-assuring.

"I'll take these pictures, write down the gender, and seal it in an envelope. Anything else before I do that?"

"I probably should've asked, but travel is okay, right?"

The doctor finishes with the ultrasound machine and turns on the lights. "How far are you guys going?"

"Just up north."

She leans against the cabinet, crossing her arms, her white coat straining at the sleeves. "That's fine. Stop if you need to stand and walk around for a bit. If you have any problems, my colleague, Dr. Romano is on-call."

"Thank you."

She steps out of the exam room while I right myself, then she returns a few minutes later with the envelope. "All set for you two to open together. And please tell Henry and the crew that we're wishing the Falcons luck. We hope they can bring home the Cup again this year."

I smile. "He's hoping for the same."

"Have fun on your trip."

"You too. That vacation sounds perfect."

"It'll be chaos, but good chaos. Enjoy the

cabin. It would be any fan's dream to run into you all up there. Merry Christmas."

"Merry Christmas," I say.

She leaves, and I stare at the envelope in my hands. It's right here. I could know right now if my baby is a boy or a girl. Instead, I press a palm to my stomach. "We'll wait for Daddy."

I slide off the table, tuck the envelope into my purse, and head to the waiting room, which has thinned out, making it easy to spot Eloise sitting in the corner of the room.

When she sees me, she stands and laughs. "What are the odds?"

"What are you doing here?"

She gives me the look, and I nod, understanding that it's not for the same blessed reason I'm here.

"Do you want me to be here with you?" I squeeze her hand, sensing today is hard for her, even more so since Conor can't be with her.

"No, I'll be fine. Don't worry."

"Are you sure? I don't want you to be alone." I have no idea what she's here for exactly, but I'll be the friend who stands at her side and holds her hand if she lets me.

Tears glisten in her eyes, breaking my heart. "I know," she says softly. "But I'm fine. You probably have a million things to do. Go. I'll catch up with you later."

I hesitate. Maybe she wants to do this alone. Finally, I hug her tightly. "Okay. But call me if you change your mind."

"I will."

I step out of the doctor's office into the cold air, then turn right back around. We might not be biologically related, but we're family.

two

Eloise

I'm sitting in the waiting room, crossing and uncrossing my legs, pretending I'm reading a magazine. I feel the eyes of the other women on me. They're probably wondering why I'm so antsy since, from the looks of their swollen bellies, I'm here for a very different reason than they are.

The door to outside opens, and everyone looks over to see who it is. My anxiety lessens a little when I see Jade. When we make eye contact, her shoulders fall a little.

"Did you forget something?" the receptionist asks her.

Jade stops and turns to face her, motioning to me. "I'm here for her."

Dawn, the receptionist, glances at me and smiles. She knows who our husbands are and that they play together. "Welcome back then."

My friend sits next to me, grabbing my hand.

"I know you have a crap-ton on that to-do list of yours," I mumble.

She shrugs. "You're on the top of the list now." She squeezes, and I lay my head on her shoulder in gratitude.

When we found out that last night's game was postponed until tonight, I thought Conor was going to quit hockey and fly home. I'm actually surprised he didn't show up in the middle of the night. But I'm proud of myself for talking him off the ledge. He's a hard man to calm down when it comes to anything to do with me.

"So, what are you reading?" She nods at the magazine open in my hand.

I shut it to see it's a *Travel the Midwest* magazine talking about the best places to see the leaves change in the fall. "Clearly something that will be useful this year."

She laughs.

We talk about the cabin we're renting and how we're hoping the boys make it home, but if there are any more weather delays from the storm moving from east to west, they'll be meeting us up at the cabin. Still, I cannot wait to celebrate an early Christmas with our best friends.

Finally, my name gets called, and I stand.

"If you don't want me to go with you, I can stay here," Jade says.

I debate the decision in my head. It's a let's-see-what's-going-on appointment. It could be premature for me to be here, but regardless, having someone in there to support me will be nice.

I hold out my hand and she slides her hand into mine, smiling.

"Back so soon? You know it's not going to change, right?" The nurse laughs, and Jade rolls her eyes.

"Did you find out the sex?" I ask, my gaze shooting to her swollen belly.

"Well, it's on a piece of paper in here." She taps her purse. "We'll open it when we're together."

"I'm sorry." I know they must both be disappointed that Henry is missing the moment they've been waiting months for. They were going to find out together, then surprise Bodhi and their family.

"This is our life. The one lots of women

dream about, being married to a professional athlete." She slides her arm through mine. "Now get on that scale. I'll turn around. Although I'll tell you, your number will be much lower than mine."

I laugh, plop my purse and jacket on the table, and toe off my boots. "You can look. I'm not that hung up on it."

"Now you aren't. And ugh, you got to take off your boots." She points at my boots on the floor.

"I deducted five pounds for you," the nurse says, and Jade coos at her. We get into an exam room, and the nurse takes my vitals. "We'd like to get a urine sample."

"Oh, okay."

"It's just to double-check for any infections, like a UTI, or pregnancy."

I want to say *yeah right*, but I take the cup and step down from the exam table.

After I give my urine sample, I return to the room to find Jade on the phone with someone.

"I had her write it on a piece of paper. It's in an envelope in my purse. Yep, I know, exciting. Oh, I have to go, I'll call you back." She hangs up as I sit back down on the exam table.

"You didn't have to hang up."

She waves me off. "You know how—"

Before she can continue, a knock sounds on the door.

The doctor walks inside the room and looks between Jade and me. "You again? Can't keep yourself away, huh?" She comes over and pats my leg. "I assume your husband is missing for the same reasons as Jade's?" She's smiling, which I'm sure is her way of setting me at ease.

The first time I came here for my pap smear, on Kyleigh's suggestion, the doctor recognized me and knew who my husband was. Not in a creepy way, but it happens sometimes.

"I heard all about your trip north. Sounds fun." The doctor continues talking as she sits on the stool, scanning her card under the computer and pulling up my chart. "I assume we can discuss everything candidly?"

I glance at Jade and nod. "Yes."

"All right. So, you've been trying to get pregnant and struggling?" I nod, and she continues. "Even women who have had three babies can have trouble getting pregnant sometimes, so it doesn't necessarily mean there's anything wrong. The body can be a mystery sometimes. But we'll do an exam today. Even though you were here six months ago, let's take another look. I know it's tough, and some women are like bam, bam and they're pregnant, while for others it can take longer."

A knock sounds on the door, and the nurse peeks her head in. "Can I see you for a second?"

The doctor looks at me and smiles. "Be right back."

She leaves, and I swing my legs around.

"You okay?" Jade asks.

I nod. "Yeah, I mean, it's not a secret. You all know we've been trying."

Conor likes to make announcements, so of course, he told everyone he would knock me up in record time. As the months have gone by and we haven't announced anything, I'm sure they all suspected we're having issues. We've been so blessed with our life together already that sometimes I feel guilty for being so disappointed. But every month when I get my period, I feel like a woman who malfunctioned, whose body is betraying her.

Jade opens her mouth, but is interrupted when the doctor knocks and comes back in.

"So..." she says, not sitting down at the computer but leaning against the cabinet. She's dressed professionally in a pair of slacks, flats, and a nice blouse with her white doctor's coat over it. "We tested your urine sample."

My stomach drops. Is there a reason I'm

not getting pregnant? Maybe I have an infection, or they found something else.

"I want to do a blood test to confirm that the results are accurate—"

"What is it?" I ask, my voice trembling.

She smiles. "You're pregnant."

It takes a beat for the words to make sense in my head. "But I'm not even late. My period isn't due yet. I thought a test couldn't predict that early."

She chuckles and goes over to the computer again, sitting and scanning her card. "That's why I want to confirm it with a blood test. If you give us the sample today, I'll put a rush on it, and someone will call you with the results by the end of the day. So I'd say we're cautiously optimistic." She types something into my chart.

I glance at Jade, whose smile could light up the Las Vegas Strip.

My blood is drawn, and she says she'll call in a prescription for prenatal vitamins. I make my next appointment, and the whole thing goes so fast that it's not until she steps out that I realize Conor missed it. I look at Jade. He wasn't the first to know, and that seems terribly unfair.

Jade stands and takes my hands. "I'll pre-

tend I wasn't here. He doesn't have to know."
She knows me so well, reading my expression.

"No, no. It's not ideal, but if it's true and
my blood test comes back positive, he'll be
happy. He'll give us shit for the rest of our lives
that you found out before him, but he'll be
happy." We both laugh because that is so
Conor. I place my hand on my stomach. Could
I really have a little one in there? "I'm scared to
hope."

Jade wraps her arms around my shoulders.
"Well, now I have to keep you distracted for the
rest of the day, so let's call the other girls."

"You have a zillion things to do," I say,
soaking in her hug.

"Nothing is as important as this. Come on,
we'll call them as soon as we leave here."

three

Kyleigh

I'M SITTING ON THE TOILET, STARING AT the stick with two pink lines glaring at me.

There is no way.

No possible way.

My phone vibrates on the counter, and I pick it up, seeing Jade's name.

I want to swipe my thumb and tell her what I just found out and ask how this happened. Not that I don't know how it happened, but it's all so surreal. I have a sleeping baby in the other room. Two kids under two?

I mentally do the math, figuring out when the baby will be born, while the call goes to voicemail. Great, we'll get maybe a month before Rowan is back in training for the season.

My phone vibrates on the counter again, and this time, Rowan's name comes up.

I slide my thumb across the screen. "Hey."

"Hey." He sounds tired and frustrated and worried.

I hate this part of the season, when the holidays are coming. There are so many obligations that I attend alone, and I don't ever want him to feel guilty. After Parker was born, the guilt seemed to pile on him.

"How was the morning skate?" I put the stick on the counter because this is not the time for me to tell him.

"Good, but I really wish I was at home with you. Parker's napping, right?"

"Yeah."

"God, Ky, if I was home, I'd have you in bed naked, fucking you so good."

"I know you would."

When I don't play along in his phone sex game, silence descends over the line. "You okay?"

"Yeah." I inflect as much elation in my voice as possible.

It's not that I'm unhappy about having another baby. We wanted another. It's just that Parker is exhausting, and he'll be walking by the time this next one comes into the mix. It's going to be a lot.

"I'm sorry again," he says. "You sound so tired."

"We're good. I'm going to take him for a walk when he gets up."

"Ky, it's freezing out."

"Well, that's why they invented coats and blankets. I need to run to the shop anyway. The dress for that winter wedding I was telling you about is done and the bride has her fitting to-day, so I want to make sure it's perfect before we leave for the cabin."

He groans. "I can't wait for a few days off. My body is beat to shit right now."

"A straight week of hotel beds and games will do that." I desert the test and go into the kitchen to wash the bottles before Parker wakes up.

"Well, Florida put a little more into their hits this time around. You should see Tweetie's ribs."

"You boys and your competition," I say, rinsing dishes and putting them in the dishwasher.

"It was Tweetie's old team. We had to."

"Even though you like the Fury players? I'm pretty sure I remember you going on a deep sea fishing charter with Aiden Drake and Warner Langley this past summer."

"Friendship has no place on the ice, babe. They got Tweetie's ribs pretty bad though."

"I'm sure Tedi will kiss his boo boos."

"Are you going to kiss mine?" he asks in that flirtatious tone he uses when he really misses sex.

I guess I should be happy he's in his room wanting to have phone sex with me rather than having his pick of the puck bunnies who flock to the out-of-town teams. I ditch the dishes. I'll do them after Parker goes down tonight.

"Of course I will. Where are you hurt?"

"Everywhere, but there's one place in particular that needs your special attention."

"The same area that's usually completely covered during the game?"

"Hey, how do you know someone didn't give me a dirty shot?" He chuckles. "God, I miss you, Ky. This has been such a long week. I was so prepared last night to climb into bed with you in the middle of the night after we got back from Boston. I was going to take Parker for the morning and let you sleep in."

"I know." I sit on the chair in our family room and put my legs on the ottoman. "You can do it tonight."

I should surprise him tomorrow morning and show him the test.

"Go to bed naked for me?" he asks.

"I like teasing you, so it'll be a surprise."

"What the hell, Landry, get your hand out of your pants!"

Conor.

"Tell my big brother not to be jealous that you've got better equipment than him."

Rowan laughs, then I hear some fumbling before Conor comes on the line. "First off, you have no idea what I'm carrying, and second, have you talked to Eloise today?"

The concern in his tone makes my back straighten. "What's up?"

"Nothing." He groans. "Fuck, man."

"Just tell her," Rowan says.

"You two keeping secrets from me?"

"Well, yeah he made me pinkie swear and everything." Rowan laughs, but Conor isn't laughing, so I worry something happened. If so, why didn't Eloise call me?

"She had a doctor's appointment today and you know it's not coming as easy for us as the two of you assholes." I'm put on speaker, and I hear Conor fall onto his bed. "So we were going to the doctor to get a check-up, and because of this delay, I couldn't go with her, so she went alone."

I frown. "Why didn't she call me? I would've gone even if I had to drag Parker along."

I hate that Eloise hasn't felt comfortable enough to talk to us about her pregnancy challenges, but then again, she probably feels as though we wouldn't understand since I've got Parker, Tedi has Addison, and Jade is expecting soon.

"I told her to call you, but she knew you'd be busy with Parker. Fuck! I just want to go home," he shouts.

"Shit, Pinkie, calm the fuck down," Rowan says. "You'll wake the guys next door and we're here, so we might as well win this game tonight."

"True. Okay, I'm napping."

"And there go the pants," Rowan says.

"Night night time, Ky, time to kiss and hang up," Conor shouts from what sounds like the other side of the room.

"Take a picture for me? Something for me to look forward to coming home," Rowan says.

"Sure, what do you want?"

"You holding Parker in our bed?"

"Done."

"Thanks." I hear the smile in his voice.

"Say bye bye now," Conor says.

"I love you," Rowan whispers. "Don't forget my surprise."

"Fucking hell," Conor yells.

"I love you. Good luck tonight. We'll be watching."

We hang up and I hold the phone to my chest for a second, knowing at some point in the middle of the night, I'll be in Rowan's arms.

My phone vibrates again, this time with Eloise's name.

I slide my thumb over. "Hey, you."

"I'm personally offended you didn't answer for me, but you did for her," Jade says in the background. Clearly, I'm on speaker.

I could tell them what I just found out. Say I'm processing, I'm freaking out, I'm about to have a mental breakdown.

"Have you gotten your hubby a gift yet? We're thinking retail therapy is in order and maybe Peeper's after," Eloise asks.

She sounds happy. That has to be a good thing, right?

I think about Parker in the other room, asleep, and run through my list of options for a babysitter. "Let me see who I can find for Parker."

"It's already been taken care of. We'll meet you at my parents'," Jade says.

"Really?" A smile forms on my face.

Reed and Victoria have become the street babysitters for all of us.

"Call us your fairy godmothers for the day. We're on our way, so get some stain-free clothes on. Girls' day out," Jade says.

The phone clicks, and I shake my head.

The test in the bathroom grabs my attention again, those two pink lines vivid in my mind as though they were in neon. But all the unanswered questions and concerns will still be there after a day with the girls.

So I do what my friends suggest. I take off my stained sweats and sweatshirt, fixing myself to be as presentable as a mother with a young baby can be.

Then I do what no one would ever suggest, and I wake my sleeping baby.

"You'll have fun with your friends," I say to myself as guilt rips through me. I should be loving being a mom, not be in need of a girls' day out.

But the boys were due back late last night

after a long travel week. So, I'm claiming today as a break for Mommy before I lose my mind.

four

Tedi

ADDISON CRIES THROUGH THE monitor, and I place my head in my hands. I literally cannot do this again.

I'm either feeding or sleeping. Or listening to my daughter cry.

My trash can overflows with takeout containers, which feels like a mom fail because I'm never cooking anything.

Then the fucking game was postponed.

I was hanging on by the thinnest thread when Tweetie called me last night to say he wouldn't be home. I tried to keep the exhaustion out of my voice and sound upbeat, but he knows me too well. And the guilt he feels for leaving this all on me makes me feel bad since he's out there providing a life for us. Him continuing to play was a mutual decision we made.

He's texted me so many times today. Before and after his warm-up skate. On his way back to the hotel. Probably again when he wakes up from his nap.

My phone vibrates, but I ignore it, going upstairs.

I pick up Addison and hold her, trying to soothe her with the pacifier. Thankfully, she takes it, and I sit in the rocker, forcing my eyes to stay open so I don't drop her and really fail at my role of mother.

I almost have her asleep when I hear our front door open.

Who could that be?

Tweetie is definitely still in Boston because he just messaged and told me he was grabbing lunch, since they are an hour ahead, and then chilling. He really means taking a nap. A glorious, quiet, uninterrupted nap that he knows I'll be jealous of, so he doesn't want to tell me.

I rise from the rocker and walk out of the room, hearing a voice whispering my name.

What the hell?

They clearly know my name and the code to get into my house, so it can only be one of our closest friends.

I tiptoe down the stairs and don't see anyone.

Our Christmas tree sits in the front window. The day after Thanksgiving, Tweetie watched Addison while I decked the house in Christmas decorations, which I'm starting to think was my last day of not having a baby latched to my breast for life.

I hit the bottom of the stairs and hear my name whispered again. I'm pretty sure I recognize it, so when Eloise comes out of the back room, I don't scream.

But she jolts back, her hand covering her heart. "Jesus!"

I giggle, trying not to let my chest vibrate and wake the baby.

She stares at me for a moment, and I see myself through her eyes, see the pity in them. She holds out her arms, and I hand over Addison, who coos at her and nuzzles closer. I'm sure Eloise is calmer than me.

"You're really not supposed to use the code unless you're watering my plants and I'm on vacay." I go into the kitchen to make another cup of coffee.

"Answer your phone then," she says, not sitting down.

"I'm raising a human, and it appears that's

going to be my entire life until she turns eighteen."

She laughs, and Addison doesn't even stir.

"It's not funny. Why don't people tell you about this? I'm just a feeding machine. It's like I'm shackled to my house."

She laughs again and starts up the stairs.

"Where are you going?" I turn away from my pod coffee brewer.

"Getting Addison ready. Playdate time."

"Hate to break it to you, but she's not going to be the life of the party."

"Just get some of your milk out of the fridge and prepare some bottles," she hollers down. "Then get your ass up here and get dressed."

"You're swearing in front of my baby." I blow on my coffee.

"Give me a break. It's not my filthy mouth she'll learn it from."

I hear her upstairs, opening and closing drawers. A few minutes later, Eloise comes down with the diaper bag and Addison changed into a new outfit. "I told you, go get ready."

I sip my coffee. "Are you kidnapping her?"

"No, I'm kidnapping you. We're having a

girls' day out, so let's go. We've got the usual babysitters. Now get your sorry ass ready."

"Can I just stay here and sleep then?"

She shakes her head. "Sorry, all four of us are spending the day shopping and eating. Plus, we have to bring Ruby her gifts."

At least I managed to get one thing done, since Ruby's gift is sitting under the tree in Grinch wrapping.

"Then you spend the night here tonight and get up with Addison while I have a restful, full night's sleep? Deal." We both laugh as I set my coffee down and head back upstairs.

I strip off my clothes, throw my hair in a ponytail, and put on a little bit of makeup. I've definitely been sporting the new mom don't-say-shit-to-me look, which I quite enjoy.

By the time I'm back downstairs, Eloise has Addison all wrapped up to ward off the cold on the short walk over to Jade's parents' house. She's going to be such a great mom someday. I'm assuming they haven't been successful in trying to get pregnant since they haven't said anything. Conor isn't one for secrets.

"Hey," I say, feeling like a jerk for complaining about being a mother when she's trying to get pregnant.

She must see it in my face because she

shakes her head. "Nope. One day I'll be complaining to you, and you'll be telling me to suck it up."

I give her a soft smile, and she nuzzles Addison again and kisses her forehead.

"You guys are serious about trying, huh?"

She answers me by throwing my coat at me. "Here." And then my purse. "I put the milk in the bag, and everything they need for the day is in there."

A sudden wave of guilt hits me. "I can't just pawn off my baby."

"Yes, you can. Reed and Victoria are happy to help. Consider it your Christmas gift."

I feel her eyes on me as I stare at my daughter. "Maybe I shouldn't—"

"You should, and you are. I know it's hard, but mothers need a break sometimes. And it's especially hard when the guys are in season and are away so much. Now, let's go." She walks to the door and opens it, and a rush of cold air pours in.

"Are you sure?" Why am I asking her permission?

Because your mind is mush from having little-to-no adult interaction.

"Yes, now come on." She waves. "And remember this when I don't want to leave my kid, okay?"

"Deal, but two hands on the baby. Tweetie would have a conniption if he saw you right now." I walk by her and down the steps.

"Well, Tweetie is in Boston, so whatever."

It's freezing out, but this is when the snow looks fresh and white in the Midwest. When it's beautiful and glowing. After the holidays, you notice the dirt in the snow, and the white flakes just aren't as magical as before.

I look at Eloise and Addison and think about the times when Addison will want to go outside and play—build snowmen, have a snowball fight, make snow angels. And that is exactly why we moved to the same block as all our friends. So our kids can grow up together.

I try to center myself and appreciate this age, but I've never been as bone-tired as I am right now. The idea of her being able to feed herself and be mobile is a really nice thought right now.

We open the door to Reed and Victoria's house, and the rest of our friends are already there—Kyleigh with Parker, Jade and Bodhi. I'm so fortunate. It makes me feel guilty for complaining.

five

Henry

I FLOP DOWN ON THE BENCH IN THE visitors' locker room.

"I just want to get this fucking game over with," I mumble.

"You know it's bad when Daddy swears," Tweetie says from across the way. "But I hear you. I miss my girls."

Rowan grunts an agreement. "And I want to get to the cabin. It feels like a lifetime away."

Conor's been pretty quiet since he blew up about the game being rescheduled last night. I thought for sure he was going to quit so he could be at Eloise's doctor's appointment. And I was about to give Coach my resignation right after Pinkie's. The whole work-life balance is a struggle this season.

I hate that I'm missing so much of Jade's pregnancy. Plus, she's carrying the load of the household and Bodhi when I'm in season.

"Okay, guys, we need to get our shit together," Conor says, surprising us all.

"I have my shit together." Tweetie cracks his neck as if he's gotten a crap sleep.

We've all been sleeping poorly because there's nothing like sleeping next to your girl, and it's been a week since any of us have done so.

Sometimes I wonder how I managed to live without Jade all those years.

"Magic told me earlier that we're here, so we need to make it count. If everything goes well, we'll all be in our beds with our wives at some point later tonight. So, let's just put all the shit we're missing aside like we do every game day and go out there and kick their asses."

Tweetie jumps on Conor's bandwagon and starts monologuing, but my phone dings with a text message. I pick up my phone to see Jade's name.

My wife sends a picture of her without a shirt, her tits spilling out of her bra.

Someone claps me on the back, and my phone slips from my hands. I scoop it up before anyone sees Jade's picture.

All the guys look at me, then at each other.

"Sexting," they say in unison.

"Sorry your wives don't send you pictures to get your adrenaline going."

"Who's to say they don't?" Rowan grins.

Conor throws his pad and hits Rowan square in the jaw.

"Man, they've had a kid. It's pretty clear they're fucking," Tweetie says.

"I know, but I don't want to think about my sister sending titty pics to anyone."

"She better only be sending them to me." Rowan shoots Conor a shit-eating grin to confirm that Kyleigh does, in fact, send him pictures.

Conor shakes his head.

"Listen, I know we all want to get home to be with our families, so let's just get ready, beat these assholes, and go home." Tweetie finishes lacing up his skates.

Nothing sounds better than what Tweetie just described, so I shoot Jade a text that says I'll be lucky if I don't skate into the boards thinking about that picture. She sends another picture with the cups of her bra under her tits.

> Fuck, you're evil. I love you.
> Watch for the sign.

"They're at Peeper's," Tweetie says, looking at his phone. "Watching the game."

Something about knowing your girl is watching you fires you up to play your ass off. Sure, I've had some shit games even while Jade has been in the stands with Bodhi. But having them nearby always motivates me to try harder even though hockey isn't my life now. They are.

We file out of the locker room, and a minute later, our skates hit the ice. I can't deny I still love the game, but if I had to choose, it would be my family every damn time. That fact has brought calmness to my game that I didn't predict. I don't harp on every missed pass or goal. Not that I've lost my edge. I'll still put someone in the boards if they cross me or my teammates.

The first period's always about shaking the nerves out of my legs, ignoring the weight of the crowd. Rowan wins the faceoff and the puck glides toward me. I take it up the boards, Tweetie on my left chirping at Ashby, Boston's defenseman. Some things never change.

Between Tweetie, Rowan, and me, we cycle, pass, and test O'Leary, the goalie, before Ashby gets the puck, shooting it down the ice, chirping back to Tweetie about his piss-poor skills.

Unfortunately, Richards, their center, gets the puck, shooting it to the rookie at the right. Conor watches the rookie as he skates closer, Conor's eyes on the stick and the puck. He's the best goalie in the league, so I'm not worried. He'll stop the goal. Let's be honest, the rookie is either going to be too scared to shoot, or he'll ignore his teammates and only have eyes on the goal, trying to prove himself. It takes at least a year for that pressure to lessen the effects on your performance.

As predicted, the rookie shoots and Conor deflects it with his shin guard. By the time the horn sounds at the end of the first, the scoreboard reads zero-zero.

The second period is usually my best for reasons I can't explain. Rowan feeds me a no-look pass that lands perfectly on my stick, and I rip it toward the goal, but it hits the crossbar.

"Fuck," I mutter.

Their guy mumbles something to me, but I ignore him.

Soon the puck is back on the ice, and Rowan passes it to me again. It's practically a repeat of the play from earlier, but this time the puck slips right between O'Leary's legs.

The red light on the net flashes and I do my celly. I place my hand over my heart and point up in the air, my signal to Bodhi and Jade that I'm thinking of them.

Tweetie and Rowan are on me, congratulating me, before we're off the ice and the second line comes on.

That one was for our little boy or girl. I can't wait to find out in a few hours when we can open that envelope together.

One more period and this game is over and I'm on my way back to my family.

six

Ruby

I'm busy behind the bar since the Falcons are playing tonight. It's an away game, but there are still puck bunnies who don't understand that the players won't be coming here right after the game. Social media ruins everything. If it weren't for that, no one would even know the players hang out here.

Not that my boys are here as often as they used to be. Now Colts players are occupying the condo units above my bar. They're fine, I guess, but they let way too many girls in the back room for my liking. I miss my quiet crew.

As I think about them, the three Colts walk through the door. The idiots lower their caps as though that makes them incognito and beeline it toward the back room, but I step in front of them.

"Sorry, boys. The room is taken tonight."

"What do you mean? It's our room," Hayes says, looking at me like a kid who just found coal in his stocking.

"It's my room." I cross my arms. "And it's filled."

Easton Bailey looks at the televisions showing the Falcons mid-game in Boston. "They aren't even here."

"Is it the Grizzlies?" Decker asks, proving once again he's the smartest of the bunch.

The Grizzlies—another set of my boys I rarely see.

"None of your business who it is."

The door to the back room opens behind me, and I turn to see Kyleigh sliding out.

"Merry Christmas, boys." She goes around me and hugs them all.

"Ruby's blocking us from the room," Hayes says like some tattletale on the playground.

"Oh, it's okay if you want to join us. It's just the four of us watching the game."

"It's their girl time." I narrow my eyes at the three men like *don't you dare accept her invite.*

Kyleigh waves me off. "Go ahead. No one is going to care, but whoever sat in Parker's highchair and broke it owes me a new one." Her eyebrows raise.

Easton holds up his hands. "Not me." He kisses my cheek before walking around me to the door.

I roll my eyes. He's way too affectionate. Gotta be that huge loving family he's always rattling on about. They come and visit sometimes. Way too nice for the likes of me.

"Wasn't me who broke it." Decker pats me on the shoulder. "Just a beer when you get time, Ruby. Thanks."

I practically growl and stare down Hayes. He pulls out his phone and his thumbs move across the screen.

"Done. New chair will be here tomorrow." He flashes his perfectly white teeth at us as though he's charming. If he weren't the league's best catcher, I bet money he'd be a model. He's gonna be trouble. I can feel it in my bones.

Kyleigh nods, satisfied, but when Hayes gets to the back room door, he turns. "You know, an argument could be made that it's technically *our* room now and all the baby stuff needs to go."

I laugh at the scathing look Kyleigh gives him, and he ducks into the room.

"They're entitled pricks," I mumble, heading back to the bar.

"Pricks you'll grow to love," Kyleigh says. "Let's remember how you felt about the Falcons at first."

I grunt as she follows me behind the bar. Sometimes Kyleigh grabs the drinks for the room to help out since she worked here for a brief moment in time. Tonight she fills a glass with ice. I watch her out of the corner of my eye. She pours a soda with lime, which is Rowan's drink. He's not here, so why the hell isn't she ordering her usual wine or mixed drink?

She looks at me and I cock my eyebrow.

"Still breastfeeding," she whispers.

Yeah, except there have been plenty of times she's had a drink and told me she'd just pump and dump. And the fact that she didn't order a drink from me when I was in the room a minute ago? Yeah, my radar is pinging.

I glance at her stomach, and her cheeks go red before she turns and goes back to the back room.

Tedi comes out two minutes later and

points down the hall. I nod, and she disappears into my office, probably to pump.

I serve a couple of guys their beers and glance toward the far end of the bar. Eloise is there. She waves at me, so I walk down, grabbing her favorite seltzer on the way. I crack it open and place it in front of her.

"Oh, could I have a water please?" She stares at the seltzer, biting her lip.

Note to self: do not drink the water on their street. Not that it matters for me since those days are long gone.

I fill her a glass of water and she smiles, leaving the seltzer on the bar and only taking the water.

Yep, pregnant. I'm not about to call her out though. It's her business when she wants to share. Still, my heart pricks at the thought of another baby joining their group.

I finally relax a little, not feeling like I have to guard the back room so hard. Those Colts boys are dumbasses, but they'll protect the girls if anyone tries to go in there. Otherwise, their husbands will beat the living shit out of some baseball players.

A while later, I catch a group of four women eyeing the back room door while sneaking glances at the rest of the room.

I step out from behind the bar, plant myself in front of them, and hold up my hand. "Nope."

"Oh, can we not go in there?" the blonde asks, doing her best innocent act.

I roll my eyes and shoo them away with my hand.

They groan, but they go, and I watch to make sure they return to their table. I catch all the girls at their table looking at me, but whatever. I'm saving them—and the boys. Nothing good comes from a bar meet-up mixed with alcohol.

The stories I could tell them.

I go back behind the bar and inwardly smile as Conor blocks a shot from a Boston player. Everyone in the bar cheers. I swear I hear Eloise in the other room. Way to go, Pinkie.

seven

Tweetie

We beat Boston two to one. Daddy and I scored the goals with Rowan assisting on each. Conor did a great job in net because Boston seemed out for blood, but that's what happens when they play the returning champs. We hold the Cup, so we're enemy number one for all the other teams. It's shown this season, and I look like a damn punching bag with fresh bruises after every game.

"Finally," Conor says the minute we walk into the locker room.

"Get me on the plane." Rowan tosses off his gloves.

"Hurry, fuckers. Shower, dress, and let's get

on the damn bus to the airport," Henry says to the entire team.

I snicker because it's not usually Henry telling the guys what to do. He's the most patient one in the locker room, so it speaks to how much we all miss home right now.

We all get undressed and shower.

I'm midway through buttoning my dress shirt when Coach comes in. "I've got some bad news, boys."

We all circle to face him, each of us partly dressed with damp hair.

"The plane is grounded." We all complain, me the loudest, but he puts up his hands. "Not because of the weather, but because of a mechanical issue. The part will be here in the morning, and then we'll get home. Sorry, guys. I know you want to get home. I do too, believe me."

He walks out of the room, and we all fall onto our asses at our lockers. Every married or committed guy pulls out their phone to message their partner. But I need to see Tedi when I tell her we're delayed for another night, so I finish getting ready, pack up my bags to be taken, and step out into the hallway.

I FaceTime her, hoping like hell I don't wake Addison. I know Tedi said they were going to Peeper's, but I'm sure they'll be home by now.

She answers, but she's not at home. From the looks of it, I'm pretty sure she's in Ruby's office in the back of the bar.

"Congratulations. That goal in the third was amazing," Tedi says.

She's saying all the right things, but I see the dark smudges under her eyes. She's tired and I don't blame her. This whole having a baby thing is no easy feat, and most of it has been on her lately.

"Thanks, babe." She hears it in my voice, and her eyes close briefly. "What happened?"

"Mechanical issue with the plane." I lean against the wall. I'm pretty sure I hear her pump going, which means her tits are out and being squeezed, but not by my hands.

"Are you going to make it home before we have to leave for the cabin?" she asks.

We were all leaving around lunchtime to-morrow to get up there, and now I have no idea. There are a lot of best- and worst-case sce-narios to consider.

"I'm not sure."

"Well, we can wait. Or I'll call and say we're checking in a day late or something."

"Hopefully it doesn't come to that." Disappointment fills every fiber of me. Right now, I'm wishing I retired last year so I'd be at home with her and Addison. I could take Addison for the night and give her the much-needed break she needs. We should probably look into getting help since she's doing all this while trying to start her business. Even if she insists she doesn't need help.

"Hey," she says, pulling me from my thoughts. "It's okay. We're okay."

Her reassurance means she noticed how much guilt rests on my shoulders these days.

"It's just a rough patch, but you'll be here tomorrow, and we have a long weekend to celebrate with our friends. And then our little girl's first Christmas—"

"And then more games," I interrupt.

"Yes, and that's okay. Right now, I'm doing most of the childrearing, but one day you'll retire, and you can take all the feedings and late nights with the next baby while I'm working. It will all even out, Tweetie. And before you ask, of course I want you home, but not to take care of Addison. Well, that's not exactly true, but I want you home because I love you and I like it when you're around." She smiles coyly. "Most of the time anyway."

"You just had to throw that in there, didn't you?"

"It was sounding really sappy."

We both chuckle.

"Thanks."

She nods, knowing it's exactly what I needed to hear. This isn't going to break us. We're good. How I ever got lucky enough to win her back, I'll never understand.

"So, you're pumping?" I ask.

She tips the camera down to show the pump attached to her nipples.

"I wish I could milk you right now."

She scoffs. "Tweetie, we've been over this. I'm not into the whole milking fetish."

"But you do like it when I suck on your tits, and your milk is so sweet." My dick stirs in my suit pants.

She shakes her head, but I remember the first time we had sex after she had Addison. She was riding me, and they started leaking. She might deny it, but she was turned on when I brought her tit down to my mouth and sucked.

"No comment. So back to the hotel?"

"Give me one more look?" I add the flirtatious tone that usually lightens the mood for us.

She tips the camera back down and keeps it there.

The longing to be with her is so great, I want to pound my fists into the concrete wall from how trapped I feel.

She brings the camera back up to her face. "Where's Addison?"

"With Reed and Victoria. I've had a nice day of relaxation with the girls."

Something in my chest loosens. "That's good to hear."

She laughs. "It's funny, because I was losing my mind this morning. Addison would not calm down, but now I can't wait to get back to her."

"You need some time away. It's good for you," I say, wishing she'd take more. I think she's nursing that wound of having a mother who didn't stick around. She feels like personal time is a bad thing, when really, it's a necessity.

"I know, it's just hard. You know?"

"I do." God knows I have my own daddy issues to deal with. Being away so much because of my job is like a slice to the unhealed wound of having a father who was never there for me.

"Well, get to the hotel and I'll call you when I get home... unless you'd rather sleep."

"Fuck no. I need to see those tits without tubes attached, and I'm really hoping you'll slide that camera down a little more."

"I will." She chuckles.

"Promise?"

"Promise." She smiles, but there's a good chance she'll fall asleep before we ever get there. At this point, I'd be happy just to fall asleep on the phone with her. "Now go and keep me updated."

"Be careful getting home," I say.

"I will. Love you." She kisses toward the screen.

"Love you. Thanks for being the world's best wife and mother."

She laughs. "Nice addition. Just get home, Tweetie."

"I'm trying."

"I know."

Eventually, one of us will have to end this conversation, but I don't want to hang up. I want to stay on with her until I'm outside our front door—which isn't feasible, I know.

"Okay, I need this suction off my nipples... Wait!" she screeches. "No. Don't." The phone drops from her grip, then she screams, "Hayes!"

"Shit, sorry," I hear Hayes say. "I didn't

know you were in here. I was just grabbing a pen. Fuck, don't tell Tweetie. I didn't see anything." I hear the door slam shut.

Tedi laughs and picks up the phone. "I think I just scared Hayes within an inch of his life. He'll never get a girl pregnant now."

"Did he see your tits?" Anger boils over inside me while Tedi can't stop laughing.

"Do you really want to know?" She cringes.

My hand squeezes the phone so hard it makes a sound. "I'm gonna kick his ass."

"No, you're not. Believe me, he's more scarred than turned on."

"Stop, Tedi." My jaw clenches.

"I just mean he's not going to beat off to them tonight or anything."

"Tedi," I say with the last of my patience, thinking about another man seeing my wife's tits.

She's still laughing, not embarrassed in the slightest. "Go, babe. Love you."

I tell her I love her, and we finally hang up. Then I scroll through a few pictures that usually get me through my time away, but this has been a longer trip than most.

Fucking mechanical issues.

Then the thought comes to my mind. Fuck

if I'm going to sit here and not take matters into my own hands.

I pocket my phone and go back into the locker room, where everyone is starting to head to the bus.

I corner Rowan, Henry, and Conor. "How about we get home our own way?"

eight

Conor

"How exactly are we gonna do that?" I ask Tweetie.

"You mean get our own flights?" Henry asks, and I hear the hopeful note in his voice. He'll do it to get home to Jade.

Rowan's already got his phone out, and I'm sure he's searching flights.

"You actually used your brain, good boy." I pat Tweetie's head, but he ducks under my hand and goes to punch me.

"Fuck off," he says.

"If you get me home and I'm fucking my wife tonight, I'll do exactly that." I grab my backpack, securing it with the hopes that I'm on my way to the airport.

Rowan's still scrolling on his phone while the three of us look on like a bunch of teenage boys waiting for him to show us a nudie picture some girl sent him. We look pathetic, but damn, we miss our women.

"No flights," Rowan says.

"Let's go to the airport. I'll buy our tickets from other people," I say.

Rowan shakes his head. "No, I mean, there are no more flights leaving tonight."

Henry steps closer to Rowan as if it's taking all his control not to take the phone from his hand.

"The movies always show red-eye flights and people buying tickets last minute to tell the love of their life they love them." I peer over Rowan's shoulder.

His shoulders twitch as though he wants us to get away from him.

"I think that's exactly it—it's the movies." Rowan shakes his head with finality.

All of us step back, and our shoulders fall.

"What about a train? Or a bus? Or shit, let's rent a car?" Tweetie throws every idea out there.

It's late and car rental places are already closed.

Rowan's thumbs move across his screen

again, and we all crowd him, hoping he's going to give us the answer we want.

"There's a bus," he says, looking at his watch again. "But we'd have to leave, like, now and even then—"

"Let's go." Henry grabs his bag.

I pick up Tweetie's, shoving it into his chest.

Rowan does something on his phone. "Uber is five minutes out."

I jog to tell Coach we're heading out on our own. He tells me we're crazy, but he's not going to bother telling us not to because he knows we'll do it anyway. The rest of our bags will be delivered to our houses when they land.

I meet the guys at the Uber and we all pack in.

Tweetie wedges himself in the middle, wiggling to find room that isn't there. "No XL, Magic?"

"It would've been another five minutes." Rowan, who took the passenger seat up front, says to the driver, "We need to get there as fast as you can."

He glances at the three of us jam-packed in the backseat, then puts the car in drive. We all bitch and complain about which parts of our bodies are going numb, and Tweetie bitches about a bruise on his ass that's killing him in the position he's in.

"Oh, can we stop at Tasty Burger?" Tweetie asks, and the Uber driver puts on the turn signal.

"No!" the three of us scream, and the driver looks to Rowan for guidance.

"We're not stopping. You can eat there. I'm sure there are vending machines," Rowan says.

"Vending machines? I burned, like, five thousand calories tonight. Daddy needs to re-fuel." Tweetie groans.

"Exaggeration." Henry coughs the word into his fist.

"And Daddy? Please tell us you and Tedi aren't into that?" Rowan chimes in from the front seat.

"Because if so, we'll have to razz you about it for the rest of your life," I say with a laugh.

"Not to mention, I'm fucking Daddy," Henry says.

"Whoa, I guess Jade must be into it," I say.

Rowan laughs, and I catch the Uber driver looking at me in the rearview mirror. This will make a great story for him if he recognizes us.

"Tickets for the bus are bought." Rowan holds up his phone and it glows in the dimness of the car.

"Man, you're really on top of your game since you became a dad. He's schooling you now, Daddy." Tweetie tries to turn and look at Henry but can't unwedge himself.

Henry flicks Tweetie's ear with his finger. "You're just sucking up because someone else is doing all the work."

"Is that what you say to Jade?" Tweetie says.

He flicks Tweetie's ear again.

"Shit, man, my earlobe is, like, the one part of my body that isn't aching right now," he says.

Thankfully for all of us but Rowan, the driver pulls up to the Greyhound station.

"I can finally feel my legs again," I say, stretching when I get out of the vehicle. I'm still tight from the game.

"I'll meet you guys there. I'm going to grab a bite." Tweetie starts toward the food court area.

"The fuck you are. You'll miss the bus." Henry grabs Tweetie's sleeve, tugging him in the direction we need to go. "And Pinkie, fuck, stretch on the bus."

"There's the Daddy we all know and love," Rowan says, leading the pack of us to whatever terminal we're leaving out of.

"It smells so good." Tweetie looks longingly toward the food court.

"I think I have a cramp in my thigh." I limp along behind.

"You guys are worse than Bodhi." Henry pushes Tweetie to make sure he's in front of Henry, then waits for me so he's bringing up the rear like the responsible parent.

"They're shutting the doors!" Rowan shouts, sprinting down the concrete walkway. "Hold up!" He waves at the driver.

Tweetie follows him, and I try to go faster, but fuck, my thigh cramp intensifies and I stumble. Henry grabs me by the back of my sweatshirt and keeps me on my feet.

"Thanks, Daddy," I say in a little kid voice.

"Fuck off," he replies.

We make it to the bus, thanks to Rowan. When we climb up the stairs, I'm assaulted with the god-awful smell of someone's food. We find seats—not together, but our rows are around one another. The minute I sit down, I pull out my AirPods and FaceTime Eloise.

"Where are you?" she asks.

I texted her earlier about the delay, but I really want to see her and talk to her. She's been dodging talking about the doctor's appointment this morning, saying we'll discuss it when

I get home. Now that my arrival has been delayed, I'd like her to tell me a little more.

"On a bus," I say.

"Jade said something about that." She excuses herself from the room.

"Is that Hayes? Easton?" I ask, seeing them lift their hands as she leaves.

"I'm disappointed, son. You let a goal in!" Easton shouts, and the others laugh.

"We're just about to leave. Everyone was having one last drink."

A drink in the back room of Peeper's sounds like a dream right now.

She walks down the hall and into Ruby's office, where she sits in the chair across from the desk. "So you guys are taking a bus home?"

"Yep," I say, thankful it was an option.

"You know that with all the stops it takes a while, right? We looked it up." She bites the inside of her cheek—her signal that she doesn't want to tell me something. "It's, like, twenty-four hours."

"What?" I yell and turn toward Rowan, sitting in the row behind and over from me. "It's twenty-four hours to get home?"

"We're gonna take this until morning, then get to an airport to fly the rest of the way," he says, all casual as if he was planning it all along.

Eloise is giggling.

"What are you laughing at, Lulu?" I ask, sinking back into my seat. "God, I miss you."

The girl beside me—who looks as though she's maybe eighteen at most—glances at me, the phone, and back at me. Then she puts in her AirPods and turns to look out the window.

"I miss you too, but you're on your way home to me."

"That I am." It's a good feeling knowing I'm getting closer to her with every mile. "Tell me what the doctor said."

"We can talk when you get home. I'm tired and you're tired."

I can't help but think she might be keeping something from me. "Okay, but—"

"Conor, you're probably exhausted. Try to get some sleep so you're ready when you get into bed with me." She gives me a small smile.

"All right. I will. Text me when you're home and all locked up. I won't bother you while we make our way there unless something happens. That way, you can be all rested for when I spoon you."

The teenage girl glares at me with a look of disgust.

"It's my wife," I say to her.

Her facial expression doesn't change.

"Who are you talking to?" Eloise asks.

"My seatmate." I turn the phone toward the girl, whose eyebrows scrunch. "I don't think she likes me very much."

Eloise waves to the girl before she turns toward the window. "I don't think your Conor Nielson charm is going to work on her."

"I only need it to work on you." I grin at her.

The girl scoots away from me as if there's any room to do so.

"It won me over, remember? And just think—you can cross taking a bus ride off your list now." She laughs.

"Except it was supposed to be with you. Remember I was going to... you know what in the backseat..."

The girl next to me gags. I guess she's not listening to anything on her AirPods.

"Okay, this one doesn't count then," Eloise says. "Now, go sleep. I love you."

"Love you so much," I say.

"I know. See you in the morning sometime."

We say goodbye, and I take out my AirPods for the time being, resting my head back and shutting my eyes. It's hard to calm my body when I feel so antsy to get back to her.

"Oh, this is good," Tweetie mumbles.

I glance over to see him eating out of a plastic food container. The woman in the seat beside him, probably in her fifties, smiles like a mom feeding her child as he digs into the favorite meal she's made for him.

I put in my AirPods and turn on my favorite chill playlist, hoping that if I fall asleep, it will feel that much faster until I'm with Eloise again.

nine

Henry

Before I fall asleep in my seat, I text Jade to see if she's home yet.

My phone vibrates a minute later. I slide my thumb across the bottom to start a Face-Time with her. She's in the kitchen, eating something.

"Craving?" I ask.

"No, just hungry." She chomps down on a chip. "You guys do know you're crazy, right? You should've just waited and flown home with the team."

"Who knows when they're gonna leave in the morning? You should be swooning right now that I'm going to these lengths to get home to you."

"I am swooning, believe me." She laughs.

"Hi, Daddy!" Bodhi calls in the background, then I hear the freezer shut.

"He's still awake?" I'd assumed he'd spend the night at Jade's parents'.

"Yeah, he really wanted to come home, but he's hungry, so we're having a late night snack." She turns the phone so I can see him.

Bodhi's in his plaid pajamas with his hair perfectly combed, which tells me he took a shower and got ready for bed, but his head never hit the pillow.

"It was a lot of excitement," Jade says, getting closer to him. "Tell Daddy about your night. I have to get my Chapstick out of my purse."

Bodhi doesn't need to be asked twice before he takes the phone and positions it in front of him, spooning his ice cream. "Uncle Waylon had us go down the stairs on pillowcases. He made a big stack of pillows at the bottom of the stairs so we'd run into them. It was so fun! Uncle Owen pushed me one time, and I went so fast."

"So we should be happy you didn't break a bone?"

"There were pillows," he says as if that makes a difference.

"I told them when this baby comes, no more horsing around like that," Jade says from somewhere in the kitchen. "Huh."

"What's going on?" I ask Bodhi, since I can't see Jade.

"What is it, Mommy?" Bodhi turns away from the phone.

"I can't find the envelope." She sounds frantic.

"The gender reveal envelope?" I frown.

Bodhi hops off the stool to help, leaving me with a view of neither of them. I can only hear their voices.

"No, Henry, the electric bill. Yes—the gender reveal envelope." I hear a scattering of items hit a hard surface. She must have dumped her purse. "Where could it be? Bodhi, you don't see it, right?"

"No," he says.

"Bodhi, come and grab Mommy's phone and take it over there," I say, desperate to see what's going on.

"Hold on." He comes back over, turning the phone away from him.

Jade shakes her head at the mess on the kitchen table. "It's not here. I mean, we went shopping, but I would've noticed it fall out when I took my wallet out my purse. I mean, Henry, it was a big envelope."

"Do you remember the last time you saw it?" My forehead creases.

Bodhi positions the phone again and walks away, probably to eat his ice cream.

"No. I showed my mom when I got to the house after the appointment. Told her she'd find out at Christmas, when we were going to surprise them. Bodhi, you remember that, right?"

He comes into view, not really searching for the missing envelope—too distracted by his ice cream. "Yeah. I saw it then. But I don't see it here." He slides into a chair at the table. "Anyway, Daddy, Grandpa said some big school is coming to Uncle Waylon and Uncle Owen's game after Christmas. That if they want them, they're going to be moving." He frowns and buries his head in his ice cream.

Jade ruffles his hair. "We'll visit them, and the boys will come home if it happens. Let's not get ahead of ourselves." She shoots me a look to say it's probably happening.

Her brothers have made a name for themselves on the hockey circuit and will most likely be going to play in college soon, which will mean a big change for Bodhi. He loves Jade's brothers.

"Let's wait and see what happens. No matter what, we should be happy for them. They've worked really hard to get that opportunity," I say.

Bodhi doesn't respond.

Jade sits down next to him and rests her hands on her stomach, shoulders sagging. "I lost it."

"I'm sure we can call the office tomorrow, right? I can pick another envelope up as soon as I get back."

She doesn't say anything. I'm pretty sure she's retracing her steps from today in her head. "Yeah, that's true. It's not the end of the world. We probably lost the ultrasound pics, but maybe they have some way of retrieving them." She smiles at me, then looks at Bodhi. "Okay, bud, time for bed."

He groans, but when she gives him the *I'm serious* look, he slides off the chair and slides up on Jade's lap, placing his hands on her belly. I tear up from the emotional turmoil of seeing my entire world through the phone.

"I'll be up in a minute. Say good night to Daddy," she says.

He hugs her tightly around the neck, then

leans down, pressing his lips to her belly. "Good night, baby." Then he turns to me and picks up the phone. I've never wanted to reach through a screen as much as I do right now. "Love you, Daddy. See you tomorrow."

"Night, Bodhi. I love you."

"I know." He passes the phone to Jade, and I hear him run through the house toward the staircase.

"You must be exhausted." I frown.

"My ankles are swollen, and my foot massager is on a Greyhound bus." She smiles, and it lights up every cell in me.

"He'll be there tomorrow night, and he'll massage more than just your feet."

"Careful there—you're on a bus and I heard Conor's seatmate doesn't like him much. Someone will think you have a foot fetish and report it to the press."

I chuckle. "Tweetie's seat partner has been feeding him nonstop." I glance at my seatmate —a guy who looks as if he'd rather sew his own lips shut than speak a word to me, which is fine with me. "Go get some sleep. I'll fill you in on when I'll be home in the morning."

She sighs and runs her hand over her stomach. "We love you."

"And I love you both. Sweet dreams, baby."

She blows me a kiss. "Only of you."

"Better be me."

She laughs. "Well, I will say Hayes is kind of a charmer." She gives me a saucy grin.

"Is he now?" I arch an eyebrow.

She nods. "A little too pretty-boy for me though."

"Aren't I a pretty boy?"

She scoffs. "You're a hockey player. You're rough and tumble. You play the hardest sport."

I seesaw my head back and forth. "Hayes is the catcher, so he's pretty badass and tough too."

She laughs again. "Are you trying to pawn me off on him?"

"Never. You're mine until my last breath."

"Better be. Good night, baby. See you in the morning. Safe travels."

"Love you, Jade." I hang up reluctantly, keeping my AirPods in and turning on some music.

Three hours later, I wake to Tweetie tapping me on the shoulder.

I pull out my AirPods. "What?"

"I clogged the toilet," he says, eyes wide.

I bolt up. "You what?"

Conor must've heard because he turns around in his seat to face us.

"What is going on?" Rowan leans in.

I squeeze the bridge of my nose. "Tweetie clogged the toilet."

We all file toward the bathroom.

"Only one at a time," the driver calls back to us.

Rowan looks at me, and we both nod. He heads to the front. I open the door, and sure enough, water is about to tip over the rim.

"Fuck, Tweetie," I say.

"I couldn't help it. I don't know what was in that food. It was great, but it messed with my stomach."

Conor shakes his head. "This is your problem."

Rowan walks back down the aisle toward us. "They have to stop the bus at the next station. And this is going to delay"—he looks around—"everyone."

"Seriously, man." Conor shakes his head.

Tweetie continues to make excuses as we all sit down.

The driver makes an announcement over the speaker, and everyone from our rows turns to look at Tweetie because they know it was him.

His seatmate pulls out a container of cookies and Tweetie actually takes one, but

Conor slides over and knocks the cookie out of his hand. "He's good, but thank you, ma'am."

Tweetie narrows his eyes at Conor. "I'm not a child."

"You're acting like one."

Rowan sticks his head between their seats. "Stop it, guys, we need to figure out a step two."

I rock my head back. I'm starting to think Jade was right. We should've waited until the morning.

ten

Rowan

I'm not really a research kind of guy, but I've had to be resourceful a lot of times in my life, so this whole trying-to-get-us-home thing has become a quest I need to conquer.

As we all stand outside at the bus station, my thumbs move across the screen of my phone. Tweetie clogging the toilet took the bus out of commission and they're trying to get a new one here, but that doesn't work for us if we're going to beat the team plane home.

"Found a rental car place that's open, but we have to get an Uber first."

"Fuck, it's cold," Conor complains, putting his arms around himself.

"Where's your coat?" Henry asks him.

"I didn't think I was going to need it, so it's in my suitcase that's probably somewhere in Boston, waiting to be put on a plane."

None of us is dressed for this weather, even though we were in Boston, because we live a posh life where we go from one heated vehicle to a heated hotel room, plane, or arena.

"Uber will be here in ten, and it will be about a twenty-minute ride to the car rental place. After that, we'll switch out drivers until we get there."

Tweetie looks at his watch. "Man, it's already four in the morning. I'm dead on my feet."

"Get a coffee. We're in this mess because of you, so you're the first driver," I tell him.

Tweetie flips me off, but we all know that he knows I'm right and he's going to be the first driver while the rest of us sleep.

While we wait for the Uber, we all go over our brief phone conversations with our wives.

"Fucking Colts were with them tonight," Conor says.

"Jade said Hayes is a charmer." Henry shakes his head, blowing into his hands to warm them.

"Hayes saw my wife's tits." All of our jaws

fall open before Tweetie continues. "She was pumping in Ruby's office, and the asshole opened the door."

"Then I wouldn't say he really saw. I mean, those contraptions hide a lot," I say.

I'm trying to appease him, but yeah—I'd be pissed too. I'm sure Hayes is going to hear from Tweetie.

A minivan pulls up along the curb with a stuffed reindeer nose and antlers on the grill. A sign on the side of the van reads GrannyGo, and I think I see Christmas lights on the inside. We all look at one another, and I double-check that the license plate is right.

I open the passenger door. "Mabel?"

"Rowan?" she says back.

"That's us."

She presses a button, and the back doors slide open on both sides. Her hair is a short bob—I'm not sure if it's blonde or gray or a mixture of both—and she's wearing a purple velvet tracksuit.

"Thanks, Mabel," I say.

Tweetie and Conor argue about going in the back, but eventually they both go into the back row, while Henry and I sit in the second row.

"So, you're going to Wheely Good

Rentals?" she asks, pressing something on her GPS.

"Yup." I click my seat belt—I think I'm going to need it.

"That's the rental place?" Henry asks me, his eyebrows quirked.

"I didn't see you looking." I ignore his skepticism.

Mabel switches on her turn signal to move away from the curb.

"Mabel, the doors are still open." I give Henry a wide-eyed look.

"Oh shoot. I'm always forgetting to close them." She hits a button, and they slide closed. Then, inch by inch, she barely accelerates as she moves away from the bus terminal. "Where are you boys from?"

"Chicago," Henry answers for all of us.

"Hey, Mabel, it's kind of late to be driving an Uber, no?" Conor asks from the backseat.

Tweetie tosses a twenty between Henry and me. "Hey, grab me a package of those cookies. Are they homemade, Mabel?"

I pick the bill up and toss it back to him.

Mabel's got a whole basket strapped to the center console with Ziploc sandwich bags of sweets—brownies, cookies, popcorn. All decorated with red or green frosting or sprinkles. None of it is in a sealed package.

"Slow down, boys, one question at a time." She glances at Conor in the rearview mirror, sitting at a light that I think we can turn on red at. She places her hands in her lap, so I guess we're not going anywhere. "It's not late, it's early. I wake up at three every morning. Do my stretching and then go out to pick up rides."

"You don't find it dangerous?" Conor continues, and Tweetie gets annoyed.

"You'll have to remember that question because it's your friend's turn." Her eyes shift to Tweetie. "Yes, they are homemade. We all get together and swap our treats, so you get a variety."

They all? There's more than just Mabel?

"But my speciality are the sugar cookies."

"Oh, that sounds good." Tweetie gets up and reaches between Henry and me, trying to place the twenty in her money container made out of a leftover container with a slot through the plastic lid.

Henry pushes him back. "You've eaten enough."

"Now now, boys, that's not nice. He's a growing boy."

Henry and I exchange a look.

"Hey, Mabel, the light is green now." I inch forward in my seat, anxious to get this thing moving.

Her hands slowly go to the steering wheel and turn with the perfect hand-over-hand technique as though she were taking her driver's test.

Tweetie keeps tapping Henry on the shoulder with his twenty-dollar bill.

We finally get on the highway, and I follow on my own GPS to see how close we are to the destination, but since we only travel in the right lane as every tractor trailer passes us, it's like we're barely moving.

We learn that Mabel used to be a teacher. She's a widow and has one daughter. She asks us if we're single, to which we inform her we are all very much taken.

"I've got a baseball player if she's interested," Tweetie says. "Likes to walk in rooms unannounced."

Henry grows tired of Tweetie's pestering and takes the twenty from him, putting it in the plastic container and tossing him a bag of cookies, which finally shuts him up.

An alarm on Mabel's phone goes off when we're about ten minutes away from the rental shop. Mabel pulls over to the side of the road, and the tires slide on the snow a little before she comes to a stop. I want to message Kyleigh and tell her I love her and Parker if I don't make it home.

"Is there a problem?" Henry asks, leaning between the opening of the seats to address her.

"I just have to take my pill. Give me a minute."

Conor grunts behind me.

"Oh dear," she says, reaching into a bag in the front seat. "I forgot my water." She puts her seat belt back on and clicks on her turn signal. "Sorry, boys, I just have to stop at the gas station and get some water. I'll be quick."

"We're in kind of a hurry." I turn to the guys. "Do any of you have a water with you?"

"No, Magic, I don't have a water bottle, because I'm not eight years old and going to school," Conor grumbles.

"Well, if I don't take my meds, you will get there much later." Mabel lets loose a throaty chuckle.

Henry's eyes widen since we have no idea what the meds are for. Having no choice but to be okay with it, we wait for her to ease back on the highway, and we all look over our shoulders to make sure it's clear. She gets off at the next exit and pulls into a gas station.

I open the door. "I'll get the water. Any certain kind?"

She waves me off and points at another minivan a few spots over. "Nonsense, Glady is here." She climbs out of the van, and we all watch her.

"She bedazzled it," Tweetie says, sounding impressed by the silver bling that reads GrannyGo shining on the back of her velvet track suit.

Sure enough, the minivan Mabel is walking toward also has a sign on the side saying GrannyGo.

"It's a granny gang," Conor says.

"Oh cute—Glady has a velvet tracksuit too." Tweetie points at a woman with red-dyed hair cut short walking into the gas station. "Do you think she has different treats in her van?"

"What the fuck is wrong with you? Do you have a tapeworm?" Conor asks, getting pissy.

"You need to eat. Want a cookie?" Tweetie holds one out.

Conor narrows his eyes for a second before snatching it out of Tweetie's hand.

"They're going to the coffee area." Henry rolls his eyes at me.

We wait for what seems like an hour for her to return with her water. In the meantime,

Conor's actually dozed off, which is good for his cranky ass, and Tweetie has put, no exaggeration, a hundred dollars in the food bin and eaten almost every sweet.

"Now you're going to have a sugar crash. That should be fun," Henry says.

Mabel gets back in the van. "Glady is having a slow morning." She looks at the snack basket. "Oh, you boys were hungry. I can go grab some more from Glady." She reaches for the door handle.

"Oh no, we're stuffed full. We just really need to get to the car rental place." There's a pleading note in my tone that I can't hide anymore.

"Of course, sweetie, let's get you there."

I relax in my seat, but my leg bounces the entire time. After what feels like a four-hour trip, we finally pull into the car rental place. I pay on my app, adding a nice tip to keep this poor woman off the road at four in the morning—although I don't think she's doing it for the money. Henry, Tweetie, and Conor each tip her as well.

"You boys are sweet. Have a safe trip to Chicago. I'd drive you that far if poor Merv wasn't waiting for me at home."

"Dog or cat?" Tweetie asks.

"Dog. Want to see a picture?" She reaches for her phone.

I let them do whatever they're going to do and rush into the rental place.

"Hi, Rowan Landry here to pick up the car you said was available."

The attendant, who looks as though he just returned from smoking pot in the back, has a confused look on his face. My stomach sinks.

"Rowan what a—what?"

"Landry," I say slowly.

He looks at a piece of paper. "Oh, you were just here. Something wrong with the car?"

I blink at him. "I wasn't just here. I just walked in. Tell me you have a car for me."

He looks at a wall that should have keys on it, but there are none. "Nah, man, I'm out of cars. This guy just came in and took the last one." He thumbs through some papers. "Landry. That wasn't you?"

"You have to be fucking kidding me!" Conor shouts from behind me.

Tweetie tugs Conor out of the building.

I rest my forearms on the counter. "Okay, listen, I am Rowan Landry, and I didn't just come in moments ago and rent a car, so where is the car you promised me on the phone?"

He looks at the board again and shrugs. "Sorry, man. I got nothing."

"So what do you suggest we do?" I glance at his nametag. "Larry."

He glances at his nametag and laughs. I assume Larry isn't his name. "There's a train station across the street. Or I can call GrannyGo for you. They're some really nice ladies. Have these killer cookies."

Henry clears his throat and pulls out his phone. "There's a train going that way that should be stopping in half an hour."

"Sorry, guys," Larry—or whatever his name is—says as we walk out of the rental place.

We both flip him off.

"Not cool, guys. Not cool at all," not-Larry calls.

We tell Conor and Tweetie the plan, and the four of us walk across the street to the train station. Maybe third time is a charm.

eleven

Tweetie

Rowan's got his phone out the minute we get on the train.

"We're going to take this to New York, then we're going to the airport. I don't care what the fucking cost is," he says.

"You do know it's Christmastime, right?" Henry asks.

The two of them have been like the parents and Conor and I the kids on this trip, but those are our typical roles in our friendship.

We take our seats and, just like when we're on the team's plane, we sit across from one another—Henry and Rowan on one side, Conor and I on the other.

"Do they have a dining cart?" I ask, looking around.

Henry groans.

The sun is peeking over the horizon, but Chicago is an hour behind, so I'm sure Tedi is still asleep. Then again, she could be up with Addison. I want to talk to her, but I'll wait a little longer just in case.

A little kid across the aisle is staring at all of us. I give him a smile and a nod, but he doesn't smile back.

What the fuck?

Henry and Rowan come up with plans for what our next move will be. Conor has taken off his sweatshirt and is using it as a pillow, leaning his head against the glass.

The kid leans over and I do the same, thinking maybe he recognizes us and he's just shy. I want him to know he can talk to me if he wants.

"My dad says you suck," he whispers.

I look at his dad, who's staring out the window. "Is that so?"

"Washed up," he says. This kid can't be more than ten years old I don't think.

"Didn't suck against Boston. Did you catch the game? I scored the winning goal in the third?" I arch an eyebrow.

Why am I talking smack to a ten-year-old?

"I don't watch the Falcons." His gaze lands on each of us. "We're Fury fans."

I nod. "Hate to break it to you, but they're not bringing home the Cup this year."

"You don't know that. Aiden Drake is the best center in the league."

"Excuse me?" Rowan tips his head to look at the kid.

"You think I'm washed up... you know Aiden is older than me, right?" I say.

He shrugs. "They're a better first line."

My annoyance grows.

Henry raises his eyebrows at me.

"You know what, kid? I'm gonna do you a solid just because I'm a nice guy, and it's Christmas. I'll be your Santa Claus today." I pull out my phone and press Aiden's number. Aiden answers since we're in his time zone and the guy wakes up at ungodly hours to do his workouts.

"What's up, Tweetie?" he says, catching his breath.

"I have a fan of yours here with me. Mind if I FaceTime you real quick?"

"Sure, where are you?" he asks, but I hang up and click on FaceTime, showing the kid my screen.

His eyes light up, and he hits his dad in the arm. Finally, his dad looks over and I give him a grin to say *yeah, your kid just told me your opinion of me. Fucker.*

I hand my phone to the kid, and Aiden does his thing—telling the kid to keep practicing and he'll see him in the league someday. Then he says the kid is lucky to have me on the train with him because I'm a great friend of his. The kid hands me my phone back and I tell Aiden thanks, Merry Christmas, and I'll call him later.

His dad nudges him, and the kid says, "Thank you. That was amazing."

Rowan and Henry are smiling like proud parents. There were days when that would've thrown me into a tailspin for a bit.

"Us washed-up old-timers stick together." I wink, and his dad's face pales.

So I'm not a saint—yet.

A text comes in from Tedi.

> Awake with Addison. I see you're somewhere between Boston and New York?

> Yeah. Rowan is trying to find us flights from New York, but it's not looking good.

> I'll call the rental place.

> Just wait until we get final confirmation. How's our girl?

> Hungry as always.

> Just like her daddy.

> Isn't that the truth.

Neither one of us texts for a second and I wonder if she's burping Addison now or still feeding.

> She's gone down for the time being. Changed, fed, and burped. Rinse and repeat. LOL

> You go get some sleep, too.

I think I will. I'm not sure I can do late nights anymore. I'm officially old.

You're officially a mother who has had no sleep for three months.

I hope you get a flight from New York. Text me no matter what. I want to know what's going on.

I will. Sleep tight, baby.

You too. Sleep on the train while you can.

Will do. Love you.

Love you.

I pocket my phone and find that Rowan and Henry are still talking logistics.

"I think we fucked up, guys," I say. "*I* fucked up. I got us into this mess."

They shake their heads.

"We followed because we wanted exactly what you wanted—to be with our families. We're going to make it home," Rowan says.

"Definitely. We'll get there," Henry adds.

I love Aiden and my old teammates from Florida Fury, but I've never had friendships like this. Guys who really have my back no matter what.

Conor's head lolls and lands on my shoulder, but I don't push him off, just let him sleep.

I'm way too lucky a bastard to have the life I do, but hell if I'm giving any of it back.

Now, I need to get home to my girls.

twelve

Jade

I HANG UP THE PHONE AFTER LISTENING to the doctor's office's recording three times to make sure I heard it right. Disappointment lands hard in my gut. I pull out my phone and message Henry.

> The office is closed until after Christmas. The voicemail says to call the on-call doctor if anything is wrong, but no one will be in the office to do anything regarding paperwork.

The three dots appear immediately.

> I'm calling the on-call
> doctor. They can go to the
> office and look in your file.
> Give me five minutes. We're
> just getting to the airport.

The boys have secured flights, but rather than come home, they're going to go right to the cabin. We'll pack their bags and meet them there. It's the easiest option. Eloise will drive with Bodhi and me, and Kyleigh and Tedi will drive together. It's not ideal, but at least the guys are on their way to us.

"Bodhi!" I call from my bedroom.

He runs down the hall and jumps on my bed, rolling around before looking at me. "Yeah?"

I have the little pink and blue jerseys out. I was going to give one to Mom and Reed for Christmas to reveal the gender of the baby. Since I'm an idiot and lost the envelope, that won't be happening, so I fold them together and put them in my nightstand drawer until we can find out.

"What are those?" Bodhi asks.

"Little jerseys. I was going to wrap either the pink or blue one up for Grandma and

Grandpa to open on Christmas. A surprise to tell them what we're having."

"Oh."

There's something in his tone I can't quite figure out. Disappointment maybe? It's probably because Henry has been gone so long, and I've been messaging nonstop with everyone trying to figure it out. The boys' little *Planes, Trains, and Automobiles* excursion over the last twelve hours has been eventful, to say the least.

"The doctor can't tell you?" Bodhi asks.

I shake my head and sit on the bed, running my fingers through his soft brown hair. "No, they're closed, so we'll find out after Christmas."

"Are you sad?"

I shrug. Very sad, but I would never tell him. "We'll find out eventually. But I'm really happy we get to celebrate with everyone this weekend. It's not a big deal."

I'm not really lying. I *am* happy to spend time with our friends and be with Bodhi and Henry for some uninterrupted time away from home.

"Are you packed?" I change the subject.

"Almost."

"Want some help?"

He bolts up. "No. I've got it." He runs out of the bedroom and down the hall.

As I'm finishing up packing for Henry and myself, I hear the door open, and Waylon calls up, "Jade!"

"Up here."

He jogs up the stairs, stopping at Bodhi's room. "Whatcha doing, bud?" I hear Bodhi's door slam before Waylon walks into my room. "What's up with him?"

"I don't know." It's unusual for Bodhi to act like that. "I think he misses Henry."

"As we all do. Your butler is here at your service, madam." He makes a flourish with his hand and bends at the waist.

I stare at him, annoyed. "You're helping your pregnant sister."

He chuckles, picks up the luggage, and walks out of the room. I do one last check to make sure I have everything and follow him out.

I knock on Bodhi's door. "You sure you don't need my help?"

"Almost done," he says.

Waylon stops at the bottom of the stairs, about to climb back up. "Oh, I thought I had to carry you down too."

"And to think there's no line of girls waiting to date you."

He scoffs. "I had two in my bed last night."

"Yeah, okay. Bags, bellboy." I snap my fingers. "Mom and Reed would never let that happen." Though he's bold enough to try it, unlike Owen.

He walks out the back door with my bags, and I go to the kitchen to grab some snacks for the trip. We've already arranged for groceries to be delivered to the cabin before we get there. The place is supposed to be decorated for Christmas. I can't wait to see it in real life. The pictures online were amazing.

Waylon is walking up the staircase of the back porch when I open the door and throw him the keys. "Pull it around the front. We're getting Eloise."

"She's not pregnant. Why am I her butler?" he asks.

I shut the door. He'll find out soon enough that she actually is pregnant.

"Bodhi!" I yell, grabbing my purse.

"Coming!"

I double-check that everything is off and the timer for the living room lights is on, then I walk out the front door, leaving it open so Bodhi knows to come out that way.

After he parks the SUV, Waylon walks up the stairs, holding out his hand.

"Oh, how sweet of you."

"Well, if you slip and fall, Henry will cut my dick off, so..." He shrugs.

I roll my eyes and accept his hand, carefully walking down the stairs. "Will you go find Bodhi and see what's taking him so long?"

He bows. "Of course, my lady."

I shake my head and see Eloise coming across the street with two suitcases. Kyleigh's SUV's engine is on in her driveway, and she's bringing a suitcase out of her house. Tedi's front door opens too.

"Waylon, bring the snack bag on the kitchen counter," I say.

He raises his hand and flips me off, slamming the front door.

"I need one of him," Eloise says.

"He's for rent, and there's another if he's not available," I joke.

We laugh as she puts her suitcases in the back of the SUV. "Where's the little man?"

"That's the question of the hour."

I stare up at the house, waiting for the front door to open.

What is this kid up to?

thirteen

Bodhi

"Hey, Bodzilla, what are you doing?" Uncle Waylon knocks on my bedroom door.

"Nothing."

He twists the doorknob, but I locked it. "You know you can trust me. I keep secrets."

I fall back on my heels, frustrated. I have no idea how to wrap a jersey. Rising off the floor, I walk to the door, open it, and peek into the hallway.

"It's only me," he says.

I open the door enough for him to slip in, then I shut it and lock it again. He stares at the jersey that's half in the wrapping paper I stole from the basement this morning when Mommy was on the phone.

"What's this, bud?" He picks up the jersey with my last name on the back and the number two.

"It's a jersey for the baby."

His eyes run up and down it. "You bought this?"

I shake my head.

"Who did?"

"Mommy."

"For what?"

"For Grandma and Grandpa."

"Shit, no way," he says.

"You swore."

Uncle Waylon and Uncle Owen swear a lot in front of me, but I never tell Mommy and Daddy. I don't want them to think I'm a tattletale.

"Sorry, so you mean your mom already knows she's having a—"

"No…" I look at the floor for a sec. "I took the doctor's envelope from Mommy's purse."

His eyebrows raise. "The one she's been searching for? Damn, Bodzilla, she's been all over your house and mine searching for that thing."

"I know." Now I feel kinda bad about

taking it. Mommy looked sad when she couldn't find it.

He bends down to the floor and picks up the wrapping paper. "So what are you trying to do with it?"

"I wanted to give it to Mommy and Daddy. I was just going to give them the envelope while we're at the cabin when we all exchange presents, but then Mommy showed me the two jerseys."

"Two?" Uncle Waylon's eyes are so wide I think they might pop out of his head. "Is she having twins?"

I shake my head. "No, I don't think so. One pink and one blue, and she was going to wrap one up for Grandma and Grandpa."

He nods. "Gotcha." He folds up the jersey and places it on the wrapping paper. "You have some tape?"

"You're not going to tell her?" My eyes go wide.

He laughs. "Hell no. I love that you have balls, kid."

"Have what?"

"Forget I said that. Mind eraser." He slides his hand over my forehead. He and Uncle Owen do that when they don't want me to repeat what they said. "She's gonna love it, Bodhi."

I go into my drawer and grab the tape I have for the poster I made for school.

Uncle Waylon wraps up the jersey and stuffs it under my clothes in my suitcase. "Now remember, when you get there, you can't let her unpack your stuff. You have to be one step ahead of her like a spy, okay?"

I nod. "Yeah. Thanks, Uncle Waylon."

He opens his arms, and I hug him. He squeezes me tightly.

"You're the coolest kid I know," he whispers.

"You really think so?" I go down to my knees and zip up my suitcase.

"Yeah. For sure. Owen and I say so all the time."

I can't believe he thinks I'm cool. I look up at him. "Thanks for helping."

He ruffles my hair, which they all do. I hate it, but since he just helped me, I won't say anything. "Anytime. Remember, you can trust me."

We get to the bedroom door and stop. "Wait, you won't tell Grandma and Grandpa, right? I think Mommy wants to surprise them."

"Nah, I won't. But I might razz your mom about the fact that I knew before her." He shrugs. "I won't tell a soul, promise. Now let's get you downstairs so she doesn't suspect anything."

Uncle Waylon takes my suitcase and walks me down the stairs. Mommy is at the bottom of the front door stairs, waiting.

"There you are! Ready?" She smiles at me.

I love her so much, and as excited as I am that she's pregnant—because she's really happy about it—I'm not sure I want to share her.

fourteen

Conor

"Fuck, drive faster," I say to Henry. "Did you take driving lessons from Mabel?"

Henry slows on the accelerator. "Sorry if I don't want to die today."

The roads are crap, and I'm happy the girls made it to the cabin before nightfall.

"Leave Mabel out of it. I might have to ask her what was in those cookies. They're addicting, I swear." Tweetie leans his head back as if he's dreaming about them.

We ended up catching a flight from New York. The part for the team plane didn't come in until late in the day, so we still beat them, which we all celebrated the minute our plane landed in Chicago. Something, maybe a little

Christmas magic, was on our side because they had a large SUV for us to rent. We flew through a drive-thru where Tweetie ate half the menu, then we started driving up to the cabin.

We're fifteen minutes out now and every minute feels like an hour.

We're filthy too. We all smell and are in desperate need of a shower. Not exactly the way I like to come home to Eloise, but at this point, I just want to see her and hold her and tell her that whatever happened at the doctor's appointment, we're in this together. We'll get through it.

The GPS says we have ten miles left. Only thirteen minutes before I'm with my better half.

fifteen

Rowan

I'm in agreement with Conor. I have no idea how Henry has the patience to drive so slowly. The roads are shit, and he probably is keeping us alive, but I want to be with Kyleigh and Parker so badly that it's an effort not to boot Henry from the driver's seat and get us there myself.

The GPS says there are five miles left. Eight minutes. I tap the windowsill, blowing out a breath. We've been traveling for way too long.

"Will you all just calm down?" Henry says. "It's only eight minutes. We've gone through so much to get to this point and now we're only eight minutes away."

They don't make people like Henry anymore, but thank God he's ours.

My leg bounces as we drive. A text comes in from Kyleigh.

> We're getting dinner ready for you guys. I hope you get this. The signal isn't great here and we can't see where any of you have been for the last hour.

"Huh," I say.

"What?" Tweetie asks.

"Seems the girls can't see us on the tracker app and they're not sure any texts are getting through."

Henry glances at me, reading my mind.

"You gonna cut the lights, Henry?" Tweetie whispers.

"Guys, I'm not playing games. I'm going to barge through that door and pick up my girl as soon as we get there," Conor says.

"You're no fun." Tweetie frowns at him.

The GPS says we now have three minutes until arrival. After another minute, we turn down the long gravel driveway to the cabin.

"Just remember we haven't been stellar

with our ideas lately. We just spent an entire twenty-four hours traveling from Boston to here." Conor inches between Henry and me. "Let's quit while we're ahead."

I shrug.

"I guess he's right," Henry says.

"Yeah, I don't want Tedi to drop Addison or anything."

We all laugh, and the trees clear, the cabin coming into view. It's lit up and as gorgeous as the pictures. Not that any of us care as long as the people we love are inside.

Henry parks the SUV next to his own from home and kills the lights. "Beat the GPS by one minute!" He raises his hand in victory.

"Pathetic," Tweetie mumbles.

"I would've beat it by five at least," Conor says.

"Then you'd be in a ditch right now," Henry argues.

We all grab our backpacks, and we don't even make it a few steps from the SUV before the cabin door opens.

Bodhi spots Henry right away. "Daddy!" He jumps off the top step and Henry instantly drops his bag and catches him, spinning him around.

"Now that's impressive. Not your one-minute GPS bullshit," Tweetie says, jogging up the stairs.

Conor's already inside somewhere—probably has Eloise strapped to a bed.

I step into the house, not seeing Kyleigh. Then she turns a corner, holding Parker. My entire body calms, and I drop my bag and cross the room.

"Hey, stranger," she says with a big smile.

I wrap my arms around her and our son, kissing her forehead then Parker's. Her hand grips the back of my jacket, and she sighs as if in relief.

Finally.

"Daddy needs a shower," she says to Parker.

I draw back and stare at them for a second, then Kyleigh. "Close your eyes, little man."

I press my lips to hers and slide my tongue through the seam of her mouth, kissing her thoroughly.

Nothing feels sweeter than this moment.

sixteen

Kyleigh

Parker is on his activity mat in our bedroom, and I stand in the doorway of the ensuite between him on the floor and Rowan in the shower.

God, he looks good. Tired and worn down, but still so gorgeous. He keeps telling me the stories of what they went through, and I really care and want to know, but the news about me being pregnant is on the tip of my tongue and pressing against my lips, demanding I blurt it out. Holding this secret for the last day has felt like a year.

"They have this grandma Uber gang called GrannyGo, and they wear these purple velvet tracksuits that are bedazzled," he says.

"Really?"

He turns off the water, opens the shower door, and if we didn't have our son in the room, I might have jumped him.

"Ky, you can't stare at my dick like that and not expect me to fuck you on this counter." He strips the towel from the rack and dries himself.

"I wish all the couples weren't having a little alone time right now because I'd ask them to watch Parker and let you fuck me on the counter."

He steps out of the shower, wrapping the towel around his waist, and cuts across the room. He cages me to the door, glancing at Parker before his thigh nudges my legs open. "We could... I mean, he doesn't know."

"Rowan." I push at his chest, and he chuckles.

"Yeah, I know, but you have no idea how badly I want you." He runs his tongue along my jaw to my ear.

Reluctantly, I press my hands to his chest. "I do have an idea, because I want you just as bad."

He kisses me briefly and goes to the sink, cracking his neck and putting on deodorant. I've watched him get ready so many times, but I've never appreciated how sexy he is. Well, I have, but it's been a long time since I've clenched my thighs just watching him do everyday things.

"Tweetie was obsessed with Mabel's cookies. I told you how he blew out the bathroom on the Greyhound, right? I'm waiting for that to show up on TMZ or some shit."

I prop myself up on the counter. He slides between my open thighs and places his hands on my hips.

"And this guy at the car rental place." He shakes his head. "He was so high, and he gave our car away. I thought I was going to reach across the desk and strangle him. I was so pissed."

"Hey, sweetie." I place my hands on his cheeks, running them down the stubble that's grown there since yesterday.

He kisses me but starts into another story. "Oh, and there was this kid on the train. He said Drake was a better center than me—"

"Babe." I try to get his attention again.

"You should've seen his dad's face—"

"Rowan."

He kisses me again and continues, "—on the plane—"

"I'm pregnant."

He stops mid-sentence.

Shit.

"I'm sorry. That's not how I wanted to tell you, but I just—" I fumble over my words, feeling even more nervous about his reaction now.

His eyebrows furrow, and he glances over his shoulder at Parker, then back at me. "You're pregnant... again?"

"Well, yeah. I already had the first one." I point at Parker.

"When did you take a test?"

I'm not sure about his reaction. I mean, we've talked about having more kids. And we haven't been careful every time since Parker was born.

"Yesterday morning. I was late and so—"

"God, Ky, really?"

"Yes. Are you... not happy?" I thought he'd be more excited. Maybe he's tired.

"Of course I'm happy. I'm just in shock. The picture you sent at Peeper's yesterday— you had a vodka soda in your hand."

I tilt my head at him.

His head rocks back in understanding. "Ah, you used my trick of soda and lime. Smart."

I nod.

He scoops me up off the counter and walks me into the bedroom, where he deposits me on the bed. Then he picks up Parker and sits down next to me.

"A family of four," he says, placing his hand on my stomach—the same way he did when we found out we were pregnant with Parker.

"Four," I say, covering his hand with mine.

Parker smacks Rowan's cheeks, and Rowan kisses his little palms before pulling us all into a hug. "This is the best Christmas gift. Does anyone else know? Let's go tell them."

I squeeze his hand. "Yeah... but hey... I don't want to tell everyone yet. I mean with Eloise and Conor trying and—"

He nods. "Right, okay, let's wait until at least after the holidays."

I smile and lean my head on his shoulder, and Parker hits my cheeks. We lie in bed with Parker between us, playing with him and enjoying our family now that we're all back together.

Until we hear Conor shout.

seventeen

Eloise

I wanted to wait for Conor to be rested before I told him the big news. I wanted to wait until we exchanged gifts so I could give him the wrapped present currently in my suitcase. I've envisioned it a million times, but now that he's in front of me, I don't want to wait another minute.

He's naked in the bathroom, running a towel over his hair.

From the bed, I admire his bare ass, seeing some fresh bruises.

"So, are you finally going to tell me about your doctor's appointment?" he asks, finding my reflection in the mirror.

I lift my legs and cross them on the bed,

fidgeting with my hands. "It didn't go how I thought."

He's going to be happy. Even after I got the phone call yesterday that the blood test came back positive, I'm still so scared it's not true, since I haven't actually missed a period yet.

"What does that mean?" He turns around with a concerned look on his face, but I'm distracted because my libido goes into overdrive seeing his assets on display.

"You're gonna need to cover up so we can have this conversation without me falling to my knees."

"Well, I wouldn't complain," he says, but he goes to the suitcase and pulls out a pair of joggers.

He sits on the bed, but I get up. He groans.

"I'll be right back." I go to my suitcase and pick up the present I wrapped this morning for him.

He frowns. "We weren't exchanging our gifts for each other while we were here, I thought?"

I shake my head and go back over to the bed, placing the gift on the mattress beside him. "It's kind of for both of us anyway." I nudge it closer.

He stares at me then picks it up, unwrapping it. After he tears off the paper, he stares at the white box for a beat, then lifts the lid. My heart races as he digs through the tissue paper, finding his bucket list. I put a check mark on number forty.

He looks up and his mouth falls open. "What? When? How? I'm so confused."

Tears slip down my cheeks. "I'm not late. The doctor did a urine pregnancy test and then did my bloodwork as a precaution, and both came back positive."

He tosses the list aside and grabs me, lifting me so I straddle him. "Really?"

I nod. "But I'm still really scared. I mean, it's so early, Conor."

My tears fall without stopping. They're from both happiness and fear. And the fact that he's finally here with me and I can tell him how I'm feeling.

"Hey, it's a good thing. A great thing. You're pregnant, and whatever happens, we'll get through it, but in this moment, we're only going to be happy about this, okay? We have no reason to feel otherwise. So, let's be optimistic and enjoy this moment." His hand covers my stomach, and he leans in to kiss me.

I dodge it. "There's one more thing."

"What? Is it twins?"

I shake my head. "No. Too early to tell that. Jade was at the doctor, and she was in the room with me, so she knows. I'm sorry—she knew first."

He laughs. "Okay." He says it casually, as if he isn't hurt by it.

"You're not mad?"

He tucks a strand of my hair behind my ear and stares into my eyes. "Babe, never. I'm glad she was there for you when I couldn't be."

I wrap my arms around his neck and close any distance between us. "I love you so much."

"I love you too, Mommy."

I draw back and shake my head.

He only laughs harder then shouts with excitement, causing everyone to barge into our room moments later.

eighteen

Jade

We rush over to Eloise and Conor's room, and Bodhi opens the door before we can stop him. I throw my hands over his eyes until I see that they're both dressed.

"Thank goodness. I really didn't want to have that conversation tonight," I say.

"What's going on?" Bodhi steps into the room.

Eloise crawls off Conor's lap, and Conor waves Bodhi over and picks up a piece of paper from the bed. He points at a line on it for Bodhi. "Can you read that?"

Bodhi stares at it for a moment, then says, "'Have a few kids with Eloise.'" He looks at Henry and me.

We step in to give everyone else room to get in here since I'm pretty sure we're all going to be hugging soon.

Eloise's eyes meet mine across the room.

"You're pregnant?" Kyleigh asks, and her hand falls to her own stomach.

Rowan is holding Parker, and he shares a look with Kyleigh.

Kyleigh crosses the room. "I'm gonna be an aunt?" Eloise nods, and Kyleigh throws her arms around her. "Oh, I'm so happy for you guys."

Eloise glances at Conor. I'm pretty sure Kyleigh knew more than Eloise had told us about them not getting pregnant. But they're brother and sister, so I hope Eloise understands that Conor needs to talk to people about it too.

Kyleigh then goes to Conor and hugs him just as fiercely. Soon, we're all in the room, hugging and congratulating them.

"Okay, I'm not trying to steal anyone's thunder, but..." Kyleigh finds Rowan across the room, and they share a look I can't decipher.

"We're pregnant again," he says for her, and she grins.

Conor's gaze shoots to his sister's flat stomach. "Again?"

Kyleigh nods.

He gets up and so does Eloise, congratulating them both. It's clear neither of them is upset by her announcement. In fact, they're all ecstatic that the cousins will be so close in age. Kyleigh starts crying.

Then we're hugging again, from person to person, happy for our friends.

Bodhi tugs on my shirt. "Mommy, I have a present too."

Henry and I look down to see him holding a wrapped present.

"Bodhi, we can open it when we all open our gifts," I say.

"But everyone is sharing good news, and I want you guys to have good news too." He shoves it in Henry's hand.

Henry looks at me and back at Bodhi. "Okay."

"Mommy needs to open it," he says to Henry.

Henry hands me the gift.

Our friends surround us, and I slowly undo the wrapping paper, seeing a flash of the jersey I had on my bed this morning.

"Bodhi?" I say, not continuing to unwrap the present.

He must see my expression because he hangs his head for a moment.

I pass the present to Henry and take Bodhi's hand to sit on the bed. He climbs up to join me. "What is that?"

He chews on his bottom lip. "I stole the doctor envelope from your purse."

There's a mixture of laughter and ahhs around the room from our friends.

Henry sits on Bodhi's other side. "Why did you do that?"

"Because I wanted you guys to be surprised. And I didn't have a gift for you for Christmas. I was just gonna give you the envelope until Mommy showed me the jerseys this morning."

I smile at Henry over Bodhi's head before dipping down and kissing the top of Bodhi's head.

"Impressive wrapping job." Henry passes it to me.

"Uncle Waylon helped me," Bodhi says proudly.

Everyone laughs. It's not surprising that my brother is in on the secret.

"Well, let's show everyone then," I say, tearing a little more of the paper. "All three of us at once."

"You're not mad?" Bodhi asks.

"No, your intentions were good, so you're forgiven. And honestly, I'm a little relieved I didn't lose it. I thought I was going crazy." I kiss the top of his head again. "Ready?"

"Yeah." Bodhi nods a bunch of times, clearly excited.

We each take a little strip and tear it open to find the pink Falcons jersey with Hensley across the back.

"A girl," Henry whispers, staring at me.

"A little girl." Tears fall down my cheeks.

Henry leans over Bodhi, kissing my forehead. The three of us share a moment. When we finally come apart, the room is empty, and the door is shut.

"Do you have the envelope too?" I ask Bodhi.

He nods. "I can go get it."

I pull him onto my lap and Henry slides closer. "Not yet." I hug Bodhi, and he wraps one arm around me and one around Henry. "Thank you, Bodhi, this was so much better."

"Yeah?" He squeezes us tighter.

"Definitely," Henry says.

I'm a lucky, lucky woman.

<h1 style="text-align:right">nineteen</h1>

Tedi

TWEETIE CRAWLS INTO BED WEARING only a pair of pajama pants. "Are you upset we don't have news?"

"No. I'm good, and one day we will." I snuggle up to his side.

Addison makes a noise in her bassinet, and he shifts to get up.

"Not yet." I kiss his chest, needing to be close to him.

"I'm on duty tonight." He kisses the top of my head.

"No, you're not. You need sleep tonight. But I'll take you up on it tomorrow," I say.

"Deal." He wraps his arm around me and squeezes me into his side.

"I brought the milk I pumped at Peeper's, so you can take the morning bottle," I mumble into his chest.

"Since you brought it up, can we talk about Hayes seeing your tits now?"

I scoot up in the bed. Addison makes a louder noise, and there's only a sliver of time left before I have to feed her.

"Believe me, you should have seen his face. He's scarred for life, so don't be worried about it. Plus, he kept rambling on about his sister's best friend that night. Remember Leighton, our nurse when we had Addison?"

"I'm gonna be honest—I don't remember. He knows her?" He frowns.

I roll my eyes. Men never pay attention. "Yeah, and I think there was something there. I remember he looked happy to see her, but she didn't."

"It's none of our business, but it's good that he wants to see a set of tits besides my wife's."

Addison wails, so I slide out of bed, pick her up, and bring her back to the bed with us. I open up my pajama shirt and feed her.

"Can I get in on the action?" Tweetie leans closer.

I push his head away with my free hand. He laughs and picks up his phone.

This is what I miss—us lying in bed, our little girl with us, doing the most mundane things together.

"What are you searching?" I ask.

"Well, we're about to be outnumbered."

My forehead creases. "Outnumbered?"

"Babe, Henry will have two kids. Rowan will have two... we only have one," he says as if that explains everything.

"Conor and Eloise will only have one," I counter.

"Yeah, well that's his problem," he mumbles, still staring at his phone.

"So what are you looking up, Tweetie?" I can only imagine.

"How we can ensure we have twins." He smiles at me. "Awesome. The chances are higher if there's a history of twins in the family. Hell yeah. We won't just match them, we'll surpass them in one go."

I raise my eyebrows. "Go to bed, Tweetie. The lack of sleep is getting to you."

He laughs and tosses his phone down, then slides in next to me, putting his arm around my shoulder. "I'll go to sleep when you do. Let's get our little girl to bed first."

I lean my head on his shoulder.

"Imagine a set of twin boys like your brothers. I'd be the king of our street. Their families would have nothing on ours when we play road hockey. Two boys. One girl."

He keeps going on and on, and I let him have the fantasy. I mean, it could happen, and the scariest thing is that I'm not sure I would mind.

"Keep writing to the North Pole and see if Santa will grant your wish," I joke.

Addison finishes feeding, and Tweetie takes her from me, placing her on his chest to burp her. There's something about your man holding your baby when he's shirtless that makes your ovaries sigh.

Damn it all to hell, I'm pretty sure we're going to have some Christmas miracles of our own next year.

The End

also by piper rayne

The Nest

Mr. Heartbreaker

Mr. Broody

Mr. Swoony

Mr. Charming

The Nest Before Christmas

Hockey Hotties

Countdown to a Kiss

My Lucky #13

The Trouble with #9

Faking it with #41

Tropical Hat Trick (Novella)

Sneaking around with #34

Second Shot with #76

Offside with #55

Chicago Grizzlies

On the Defense

Something like Hate
Something like Lust
Something like Love

Kingsmen Football Stars

False Start

You Had Your Chance, Lee Burrows

You Can't Kiss the Nanny, Brady Banks

Over My Brother's Dead Body, Chase Andrews

Modern Love

Charmed by the Bartender

Hooked by the Boxer

Mad about the Banker

Single Dads Club

Real Deal

Dirty Talker

Sexy Beast

Hollywood Hearts

Mister Mom

Animal Attraction

Domestic Bliss

Bedroom Games

Cold as Ice

On Thin Ice

Break the Ice

Chicago Law

Smitten with the Best Man

Tempted by my Ex-Husband

Seduced by my Ex's Divorce Attorney

Blue Collar Brothers

Flirting with Fire

Crushing on the Cop

Engaged to the EMT

White Collar Brothers

Sexy Filthy Boss

Dirty Flirty Enemy

Wild Steamy Hook-up

The Rooftop Crew

My Bestie's Ex

A Royal Mistake

The Rival Roomies

Our Star-Crossed Kiss

The Do-Over

A Co-Workers Crush

The Baileys

Lessons from a One-Night Stand

Advice from a Jilted Bride

Birth of a Baby Daddy

Operation Bailey Wedding (Novella)

Falling for My Brother's Best Friend

Demise of a Self-Centered Playboy

Confessions of a Naughty Nanny

Operation Bailey Babies (Novella)

Secrets of the World's Worst Matchmaker

Winning my Best Friend's Girl

Rules for Dating Your Ex

Operation Bailey Birthday (Novella)

The Greene Family

My Twist of Fortune

My Beautiful Neighbor

My Almost Ex

My Vegas Groom

A Greene Family Summer Bash (Novella)

My Sister's Flirty Friend

My Unexpected Surprise

My Famous Frenemy

A Greene Family Vacation (Novella)

My Scorned Best Friend

My Fake Fiancé

My Brother's Forbidden Friend

A Greene Family Christmas (Novella)

Lake Starlight

The Problem with Second Chances

The Issue with Bad Boy Roommates

The Trouble with Runaway Brides

The Drawback of Single Dads

The Complication with the Best Man

Plain Daisy Ranch

One Last Summer

The One I Left Behind

The One I Stood Beside

The One I Didn't See Coming

Chasing Forever

Chasing Love

Chasing Home

Love in Apartment 3B

Hit or Miss

Three's A Crowd

Good on Paper

The Abbott Brothers

Rent a Husband

Buy a Boyfriend

Standalones

Don't Mind if "I Do"

Holiday Romances

Single and Ready to Jingle

Claus and Effect

Merry Kissmas

Yule Be Mine

about piper & rayne

Piper Rayne is a *USA Today* Bestselling Author duo who write "heartwarming humor with a side of sizzle" about families, whether that be blood or found. They both have e-readers full of one-clickable books, they're married to husbands who drive them to drink, and they're both chauffeurs to their kids. Most of all, they love hot heroes and quirky heroines who make them laugh, and they hope you do, too!